IT'S RAINING, IT'S POURING

IT'S RAINING, IT'S POURING

by **Kin Eagle**

illustrated by **Rob Gilbert**

ini Charlesbridge

Special thanks to Kim and Dan Adlerman without whose
help this book would not have been possible
—R.G.

Text copyright © 1994 by Kin Eagle
Illustrations copyright © 1994 by Rob Gilbert
All rights reserved, including the right of reproduction in
whole or in part in any form.

Charlesbridge and colophon are registered trademarks
of Charlesbridge Publishing, Inc.

Published by Charlesbridge
85 Main Street
Watertown, MA 02472
(617) 926-0329
www.charlesbridge.com

Library of Congress Cataloging-in-Publication Data
Eagle, Kin, 1964-
It's raining, it's pouring / written by Kin Eagle ; illustrated by Rob Gilbert.
p.   cm.
Summary: This expanded version of the nursery rhyme "It's raining, it's pouring"
shows what happens to the old man in all kinds of weather.
[1. Weather—Fiction. 2. Stories in rhyme.] I. Gilbert, Roby, ill. II. Title.
PZ8.3.E112515It 1994
[E]—dc20   93-40897
ISBN-13: 978-1-879085-88-6; ISBN-10: 1-879085-88-7 (reinforced for library use)
ISBN-13: 978-1-879085-71-8; ISBN-10: 1-879085-71-2 (softcover)
Printed in China
(hc) 10 9 8 7 6
(sc) 15 14 13 12 11
Illustrations done in watercolors and Dr. Martin's dyes.
Display type and text type set in Goudy Old Style Bold and 15-point Windsor Light
Concept, package, book production and design by THE KIDS AT OUR HOUSE

For my parents
—K.E.

For Mao, Poppy, and Georgia
—R.G.

It's raining, it's pouring,
the old man is snoring.

He bumped his head
when he went to bed
and couldn't get up in the morning.

It's cloudy, it's breezy,
the old man is sneezy.

He blew so hard
that he moved the stars,
but of course that wasn't easy!

It's snowing, it's blowing,
the old man is growing.

He ate so much
one day for lunch
every part of him was showing.

It's warm out and sunny.
The old man loves honey.

He tried to seize
a batch from the bees
and they didn't find it funny.

It's cool, damp, and chilly.
The old man's name is Willy.

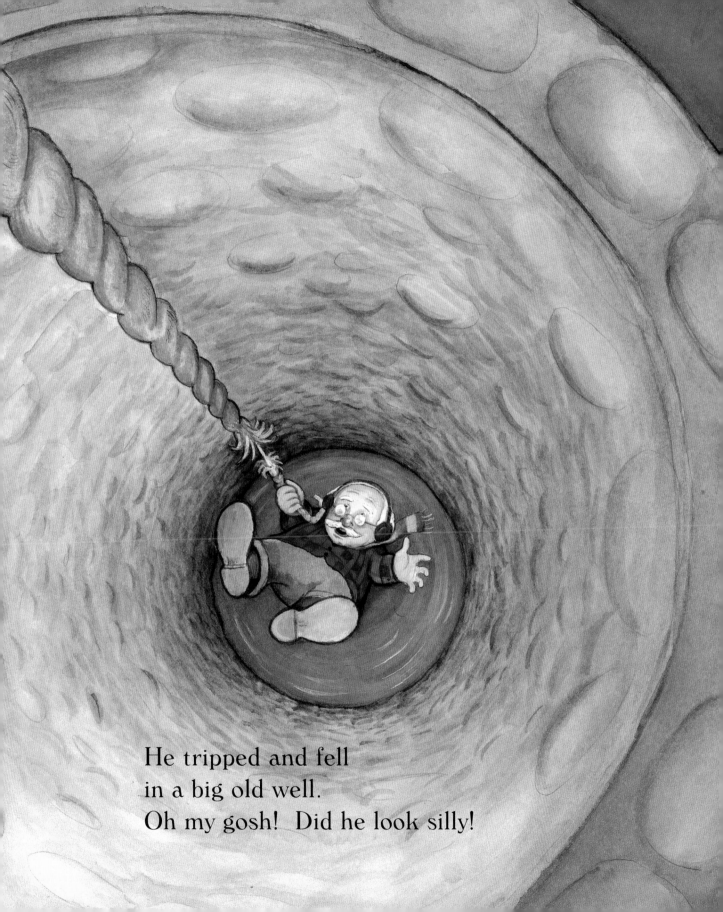

He tripped and fell
in a big old well.
Oh my gosh! Did he look silly!

It's gusty, it's windy.
The old man's wife is Cindy.

With ants in their pants
they started to dance,
and ended up doing the Lindy.

Whatever the season—
cloudy, sunny, breezin'—
if he gets to bed
without bumping his head,
then the old man thinks it's pleasin'.

It's Raining, It's Pouring

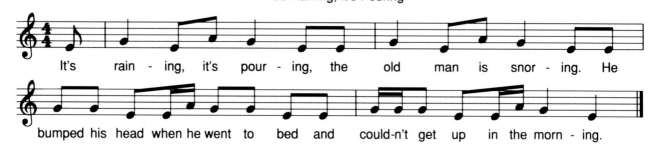

It's rain-ing, it's pour-ing, the old man is snor-ing. He bumped his head when he went to bed and could-n't get up in the morn-ing.

2. It's cloudy, it's breezy,
the old man is sneezy.
He blew so hard
that he moved the stars,
but of course *that* wasn't easy!

3. It's snowing, it's blowing,
the old man is growing.
He ate so much
one day for lunch
every part of him was showing.

4. It's warm out and sunny.
The old man loves honey.
He tried to seize
a batch from the bees
and they didn't find it funny.

5. It's cool, damp, and chilly.
The old man's name is Willy.
He tripped and fell
in a big old well.
Oh my gosh! Did he look silly!

6. It's gusty, it's windy.
The old man's wife is Cindy.
With ants in their pants
they started to dance,
and ended up doing the Lindy.

7. Whatever the season–
cloudy, sunny, breezin'–
if he gets to bed
without bumping his head,
then the old man thinks it's pleasin'.